W9-BFH-921

For the baby

BOMC offers recordings and compact discs,
cassettes and records.For information and catalog
write to BOMR, Camp Hill, PA 17012.

Copyright © 1981 by Janet and Allan Ahlberg
All rights reserved

PEEK-A-BOO!

by

Janet & Allan Ahlberg

PUFFIN BOOKS

Here's a little baby
One, two, three
Stands in his crib
What does he see?

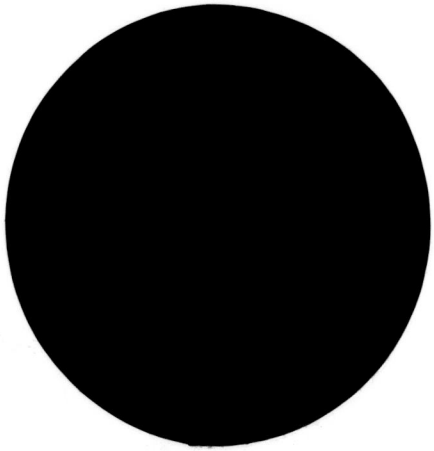

PEEK-A-BOO!

He sees his father sleeping
  In the big brass bed
And his mother too
  With a hairnet on her head.

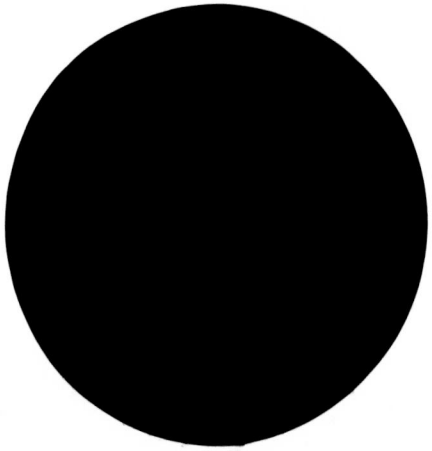

He sees the shadows moving
  On the bedroom wall
And the sun at the window
  And his teddy
  And his ball.

Here's a little baby
One, two, three
Sits in his high chair
What does he see?

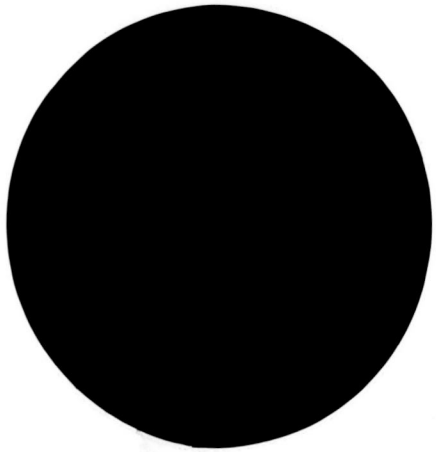

PEEK-A-BOO!

He sees his mother pouring
  Hot porridge in a bowl
And his father in the doorway
  With a bucketful of coal.

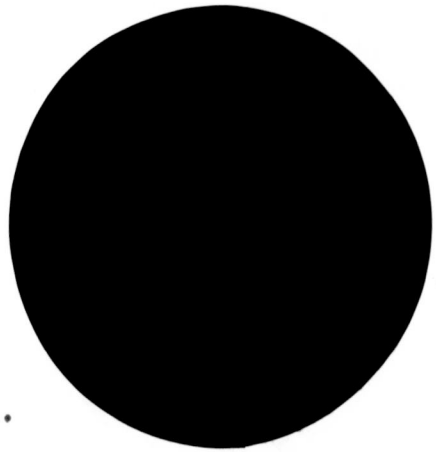

He sees his sisters skipping
  In the yard outside
And his grandma pegging washing
  On the clothes-line
  To be dried.

OXO

Here's a little baby
One, two, three
Sits in his stroller
What does he see?

PEEK-A-BOO!

He sees a bonfire smoking
  Pigeons in the sky
His mother cleaning windows
  A dog going by.

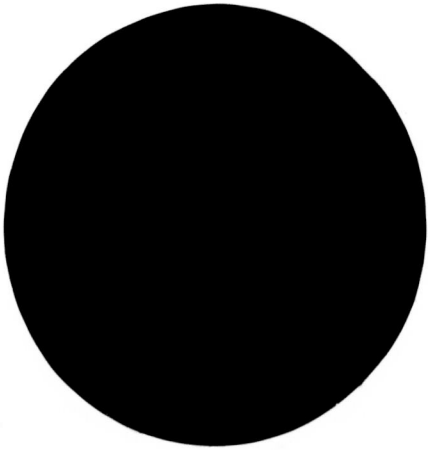

He sees his sisters searching
  For a jar or tin
To take up to the park
  And catch fishes in.

Brooke Bond Tea
AL
RES

Here's a little baby
One, two, three
Sits on the grass
What does he see?

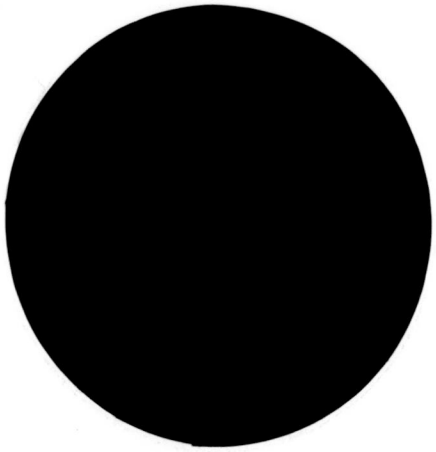

PEEK-A-BOO!

He sees his sisters fishing
With a brown stocking net
And dresses tucked in knickers
And legs shiny wet.

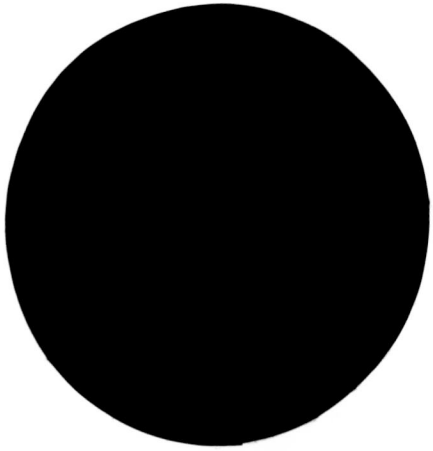

He sees the tassels blowing
On his grandma's shawl
And the fringe on the stroller
And his teddy
And his ball.

TIZER

Here's a little baby
One, two, three
Sits on his sister's lap
What does he see?

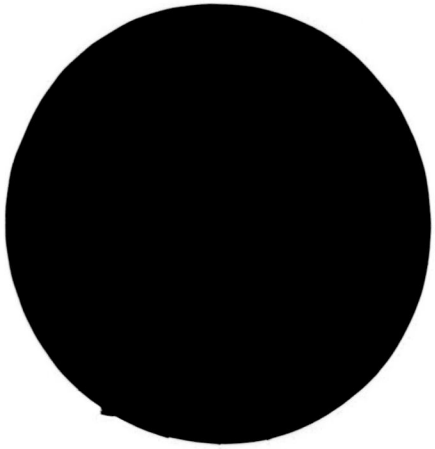

PEEK-A-BOO!

He sees his grandma ironing
His father pouring tea
His other sister squabbling
She wants him on *her* knee.

He sees his mother dozing
In the easy chair
And a dog in the doorway
Who shouldn't be there.

Here's a little baby
One, two, three
Sits in his bath-tub
What does he see?

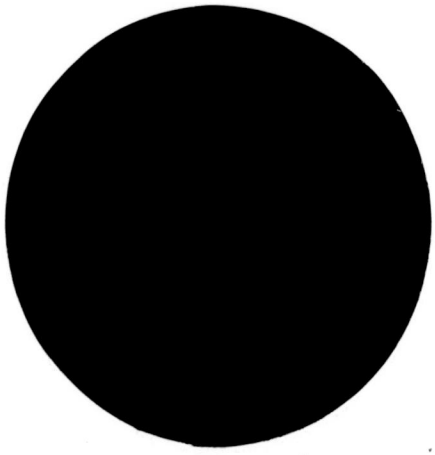

PEEK-A-BOO!

He sees his father kneeling
With his sleeves rolled up
And the flannel on the table
And the soap
In a cup.

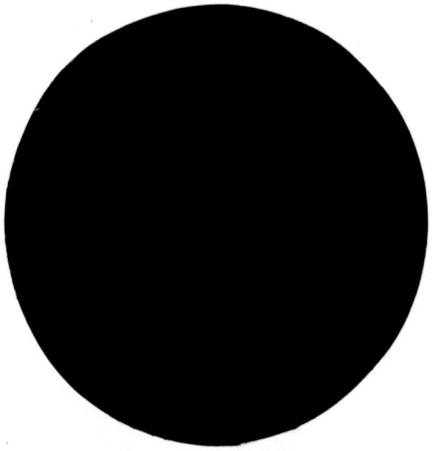

He sees his nightie warming
On the oven door
His sisters in the clothes-horse
Puddles on the floor.

Here's a little baby
One, two, three
On his way to bed
What does he see?

PEEK-A-BOO!

He sees the landing mirror
With its rainbow rim
And a mother with a baby
Just like him.

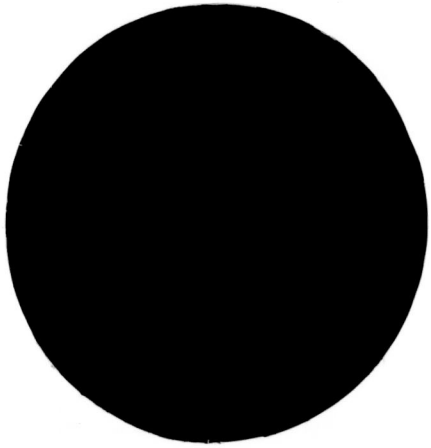

He sees the bedroom door
The crib made ready
His father kissing him goodnight
His ball
And his teddy.

Here's a little baby
  One, two, three
Fast asleep and dreaming
  What did he see?

THE END